MOMMIES and DADDIES

are

NURSES

Be Inspired !

Eileen Wasson RN + Angela Shea

AuthorHouse™
1663 Liberty Drive
Bloomington, IN 47403
www.authorhouse.com
Phone: 1-800-839-8640

First published by AuthorHouse 07/18/2011

ISBN: 978-1-4634-3451-9 (sc)

Library of Congress Control Number: 2011911497

Printed in the United States of America

Any people depicted in stock imagery provided by Thinkstock are models,
and such images are being used for illustrative purposes only.
Certain stock imagery © Thinkstock.

This book is printed on acid-free paper.

authorHOUSE®

Dedication

This book is dedicated to our supportive families and to all the nurses who leave their children each day to work tirelessly caring for others in this amazing profession. A very special recognition to the Trauma Neuro ICU and Lehigh Valley Hospital who have inspired us to be the nurses we are today.

Mommies and daddies are nurses
you can be one too.

Nurses save lives everyday
and here is what they do.

A camp nurse gives you first aid getting you back to your activities so you'll be glad you stayed.

A helicopter nurse flies all around
helping hurt people lying on
the ground.

A home care nurse drives in a car and comes to see you wherever you are.

A hospital nurse keeps a chart and uses a stethoscope to hear a beating heart.

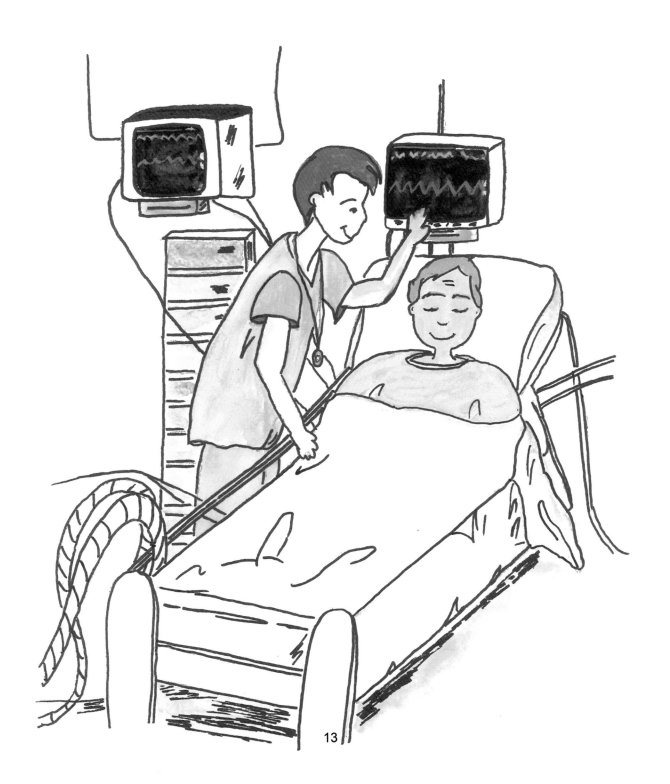

A military nurse takes command
to help the people who protect
our land.

A nursery room nurse cares for babies that cry
and makes them feel all warm and dry.

An operating room nurse will hold your hand

as you drift off to a sleepy land.

A nurse practitioner checks you from head to toe
keeping your body healthy as you discover and grow.

A school nurse teaches you to
become aware
of your growing body and how to give
it care.

To become a nurse you must
be smart
and go to college to get your start.
Study hard, don't hesitate
and become a nurse because it
is great!

Nurses can do anything as you can see.

What kind of nurse would you like to be?

CPSIA information can be obtained
at www.ICGtesting.com
Printed in the USA
248333LV00002B

9781463434519